P9-DFL-717

HOOK SHOT HERO

THE #1
SPORTS SERIES
FOR KIDS

HOOK SHOT HERO

A *Nothin' But Net* Sequel

LITTLE, BROWN AND COMPANY
New York Boston

Copyright © 2011 by Matt Christopher Royalties, Inc.

All rights reserved. Except as permitted under the U.S. Copyright Act of 1976, no part of this publication may be reproduced, distributed, or transmitted in any form or by any means, or stored in a database or retrieval system, without the prior written permission of the publisher.

Little, Brown and Company

Hachette Book Group
237 Park Avenue, New York, NY 10017
Visit our website at www.lb-kids.com

www.mattchristopher.com

Little, Brown and Company is a division of Hachette Book Group, Inc. The Little, Brown name and logo are trademarks of Hachette Book Group, Inc.

The publisher is not responsible for websites (or their content) that are not owned by the publisher.

First Edition: May 2011

The characters and events portrayed in this book are fictitious. Any similarity to real persons, living or dead, is coincidental and not intended by the author.

Matt Christopher® is a registered trademark of Matt Christopher Royalties, Inc.

Text written by Stephanie True Peters

Library of Congress Cataloging-in-Publication Data

Peters, Stephanie True, 1965–

Hook shot hero / Matt Christopher ; [text by Stephanie Peters]. — 1st ed.
p. cm.
Summary: When Tim Daniels, now fourteen, returns to Camp Wickasaukee, he serves as mentor to three rookie basketball players, continues to work on keeping his short stature from getting in his way, faces a bully, and gets help from NCAA player Dick Dunbar.
ISBN 978-0-316-10296-4
[1. Basketball — Fiction. 2. Camps — Fiction. 3. Mentoring — Fiction. 4. Self-confidence — Fiction. 5. Friendship — Fiction.] I. Christopher, Matt. II. Title.
PZ7.P441835Hoo 2011
[Fic] — dc22

2010041542

10 9 8 7 6 5 4 3 2 1

CWO

Printed in the United States of America

HOOK SHOT HERO

Yo, Daniels! Think fast!"

Tim Daniels dropped his sleeping bag and whipped around just in time to catch the basketball. He grinned when he saw who had thrown it.

"Dick Dunbar! I can't believe you're back here at Camp Wickasaukee!" Tim lobbed the ball back.

Dick, starting center for one of the best college teams in the country, plucked it one-handed out of the air and palmed it by his side. "'Course I'm back. Why wouldn't I be?"

Tim rolled his eyes. "Uh, gee, I dunno!

1

Because you're the hottest NBA prospect in the universe? You should be sitting by the phone, waiting for the offers to pour in!"

Dick tossed the ball over his head and caught it with the other hand. "Maybe I'll enter the draft after I graduate next year."

"*Maybe?*" Tim echoed incredulously.

Dick gave a short laugh. "Yeah, maybe. Don't get me wrong, Tim. I love playing basketball, but there's more to life. I'm not ready to put all my eggs in one basket." He dribbled twice and added, "Even if the egg is a basketball and the basket is a hoop ten feet above the ground!"

"Hey, Tim, you gonna get the rest of your stuff or what?" Billy Futterman, Tim's best friend, called. Billy's mother had driven them to camp; Tim's remaining belongings were still in the trunk of her car.

"Be right there!" Tim called. To Dick, he said, "So, I'll see you around camp, right?"

"Just try to avoid me!" Dick replied. He

shot Tim with a finger gun and sauntered off. Tim hurried back to the Futtermans' car.

"Thanks again for the ride, Mrs. F.," Tim remembered to say as he pulled out his gear.

Mrs. Futterman peered anxiously into the empty trunk. "Now, you boys are sure you remembered everything? Maybe we should look over—"

Billy cut her off. "Mom, we double-checked everything before we packed up the car this morning. And before you ask, yes, I have plenty of self-addressed stamped post-cards, and yes, I promise to write you and Dad every other day! Come on, Tim," he added, picking up his belongings and heading toward a two-story cabin marked EAGLES NEST. "We better hurry if we don't want a couple of newbies to grab our bunk."

Tim hid a smile as he shouldered his bags. To hear Billy talk, you'd think he'd been coming to Camp Wickasaukee his whole life instead of this being his second summer.

And what a difference a year made! Last summer, Billy moaned about everything, from mosquito bites and the lack of video games to his sunburn, the rigorous basketball practices, and the pranks the other campers played on him.

Not that Tim blamed him for that last complaint. A few of the pranks, like running a pair of Billy's oversized underpants up the flagpole and putting shaving cream on his pillow, were pretty rotten things to do to a homesick guy.

Tim had been the victim of a few nasty jokes, too. The worst was when he'd gotten a "kiss" from a whoopee cushion instead of the pretty girl he thought he was smooching!

He and Billy had gotten their revenge, however. In the dead of night, they'd pulled the classic hand-in-warm-water trick on the chief prankster, Mike Gruber. Mike woke up to discover he'd wet his bed, a fact his cabinmates had never let him forget.

I wonder if Mike's back this year, Tim

thought as he pushed open the door to the Eagles Nest. He got his answer a second later.

"Oh, jeez, look what the cat dragged in." Mike was stretched out on a beat-up old couch. Perched on one arm of the couch was another camper from last summer, Brian Kelly. The two exchanged loaded looks and smirked.

A third boy, Donnie DeGeronimo, rose from a nearby chair. "Dude, let me give you a hand with that," he said. Donnie was one of the tallest fourteen-year-olds Tim had ever met. Judging by the new low pitch of his voice and the shadow of a mustache above his upper lip, Donnie had matured a lot in the past year. Compared with him, Tim sounded like one of those singing cartoon chipmunks!

Donnie and Tim found Billy unrolling his sleeping bag onto one of the beds in room sixteen. "When you're done, come down to the court," Donnie said, dropping Tim's bag and

5

heading for the hallway. "We'll get a pickup game going with the other guys."

"I'll be there," Tim promised. After Donnie left, he turned to Billy. "You want in on the game?"

"Nah, I'm heading to the waterfront."

Tim nodded. Last year, both he and Billy had participated in Camp Wickasaukee's basketball program. But Billy hadn't liked it very much. So this time around, he was focusing on earning his junior lifeguard certification. It made sense because he was a natural in the water. Tim liked to swim, too, but he was so skinny that it took all his energy just to stay afloat. Billy was bigger and wider—although some of his weight, Tim noticed as Billy changed his T-shirt, had turned into muscle since last summer. Tim wondered if that meant that Billy, like Donnie, was maturing physically.

He also wondered—for the millionth time—when he, too, might see some changes to his own physique. He wasn't concerned with his weight, but he'd grown only an inch during his eighth-grade year. Was he doomed to be a shrimp forever? And if so, could he really be competitive against taller basketball players like Donnie?

"Hey, Daniels, you coming to play or not?" Donnie called from the floor below.

Guess I'm about to find out, Tim thought. He hopped off the bed and hurried to join the others.

2

The Eagles Nest basketball players gathered at one of the several outdoor courts on the grounds of Camp Wickasaukee. There was an indoor gymnasium, too, but it was used only when it was raining or when the boys' and girls' camps met for a social. It was at one such dance that Tim had received his "kiss."

He grimaced as the memory of that embarrassing moment flashed through his mind.

A curly-haired man with dark eyes caught his look and laughed. "Whoa, did you eat something nasty, or is that your game face?"

"Hey, Tito!" Tim greeted. "Are you our counselor again this year?"

Tito threw a muscular arm around Tim's shoulders. "Yeah, I drew the short straw and so got stuck with you punks," he deadpanned. "Come on, we're about to choose sides."

Tim counted nine players waiting at the court. Dick was there, too, as was Jody, another counselor from the year before. Tim knew most of the players, but a few were strangers. They might be new to the camp, since they didn't seem to know one another or anyone else. Plus, they were casting hopeful looks at Mike Gruber, Brian Kelly, and two other boys. But Mike and his crew were too busy laughing about old times to be bothered with them.

Tim understood how the newbies felt. He'd wanted to be a part of that "in" group so badly the previous year that he'd almost turned his back on Billy just so they'd accept him. Well, he wouldn't make that mistake again this year. And he decided he wouldn't let the new campers waste their time trying to get in good with them; if those boys wanted to be your friend, they'd come to you. It didn't work the other way around!

Tim walked up to the closest newcomer and stuck out his hand. "Hi, I'm Tim Daniels," he said. "You a first-timer here at Wicky?"

The boy nodded and introduced himself as Sam Livingston. Sam was about Tim's height, with a buzz cut and a sprinkling of freckles across his nose.

"Let me guess," Tim said, "you play guard back home. Right?"

"Shooting guard," Sam acknowledged.

Tim grinned. "I play point. Maybe we'll be paired up on the court."

"That'd be cool." The two bumped fists and then turned to Tito, who was clapping for attention.

"Jody and I feel like getting our game on," the counselor said, "so we'll be captains and pick our players."

One of the new campers pointed at Dick. "Is he going to play, too?"

"Nope," Tito answered. "He's here to observe each of you. That way, we'll know what you need to work on to become better players." He motioned to Jody. "You'll be skins, so you can choose first."

"Mike Gruber," Jody said without hesitation. Mike peeled off his shirt and planted himself next to Jody, a smug expression on his face.

Tito surveyed the remaining choices. His eyes stayed on Tim for a long moment, but he ended up choosing Donnie. He selected Tim in the next round, though, and Sam in the one after that. When all the players were on a team, positions were assigned, and the game began.

Tim played point guard opposite Mike. They found spots around the center circle, where Donnie and Bobby Last, another tall eighth grader, faced each other for the tip-off.

Dick acted as ref and lofted the ball between them. Donnie leaped just a bit higher than Bobby and tapped the ball into Tim's waiting hands.

Tim took off, dribbling toward the basket. Mike dogged him every step, clearly hoping Tim would make a mistake. But Tim kept his cool—and his dribble.

Not this summer, Gruber! he thought as he reached the top of the key. He turned to shield the ball while he looked for an open man. Merrick "Cue Ball" Jones, a lanky forward with a shaved head, cut to the hoop with his arm raised. Tim hit him with a pass. Cue Ball caught the ball, spun, and shot. Two points!

"Yow, that was so sweet, I'm getting a cavity!" Cue Ball crowed.

Tim and his teammates laughed as they raced to the opposite end of the court. Mike brought the ball down fast and drove in to the hoop. Donnie slid across the baseline to challenge him. When Mike jumped for a layup, Donnie jumped with him.

Whap! Donnie denied the basket with a powerful block. Mike reeled back dramatically and looked at Dick. But the block had been clean, so no foul was called.

Sam snared the ball on a bounce and found Tim waiting near the sideline. Tim dribbled quickly, but Mike caught up to him just as he crossed the center line. Tim drew up short and bounced a pass to Tito. Tito sent it to Cue Ball, who immediately relayed it to Donnie at the low post. Donnie jumped high and finger-rolled the ball into the hoop.

"Moses, smell those roses!" Cue Ball bellowed.

The comment was pure nonsense but uttered with such glee that Tim and his teammates cracked up. They stopped laughing when the "skins" sent a long bomb to Jody, who was waiting under the hoop. Jody was well over six-and-a-half-feet tall. He slammed the ball two-handed through the basket, drawing cheers and whistles from both shirts and skins.

Tim inbounded the ball to Sam, and the action moved back to the other end. Elijah, another newcomer, sprang forward to challenge Sam at the corner of the key. Sam panicked and stopped his dribble, a classic mistake since now he was forced to pass or shoot.

Tim darted forward to help out. Sam dished the ball to him. Tim took two dribbles and then set himself up for a jump shot.

It wasn't a shot he'd have attempted the year before, because more often than not, it would have ended as an air ball. But he'd been working hard to improve his shooting since the past summer and had gained confidence in his ability.

That confidence didn't help him now. As he went up, Mike sailed across the paint and practically stuffed the ball down his throat!

3

Thud! Tim went down so hard his teeth rattled. Sam helped him to his feet and asked him if he was okay. Tim waved the question away. His tailbone felt bruised, but he was more embarrassed than hurt.

"Daniels, take a seat!" Tito called. "It's time for subs anyway."

Tim left the court but noticed that Jody didn't replace any of his players. He filled a cup with water from a big jug and sat down gingerly. The bench was empty except for a new member of the Eagles Nest cabin. Tim felt the boy's eyes on him. He drank half his water and poured the rest over his head to cool off before acknowledging him.

The boy said his name was Jordan. "I was in the Cubs Cave last year, so you probably don't remember me," he added, referring to a cabin for younger campers. "But I remember you."

"Me?" Tim asked as he wiped water out of his eyes. "Why?"

"You were the one who air-balled the last-minute foul shot that would have sent the game against Camp Chickasaw into overtime," Jordan said matter-of-factly. "Instead, you guys blew it and Wickasaukee lost an inter-camp match for the first time in ten years."

Tim stared at him. As hard as he'd worked on his jump shot in the past year, he'd worked even harder to drive that memory from his brain. And now here he was, being reminded of it by an eyewitness—and on the first day of camp, too!

His insides burned with shame. He wanted to tell Jordan to shut up. But what would be the point of getting upset about something that had happened a year ago? So he swallowed hard and muttered, "Yeah, well, we've all botched plays on the court, haven't we?"

"I know I have!" Jordan agreed with a mirthless laugh. "Last summer, I bricked a layup with so much force that it rebounded fifteen feet off the glass!"

Tim smiled at the boy's honesty. He raised his empty cup. "Here's to saving bricks for building walls!"

"Hear, hear!" Jordan said.

They turned their attention back to the game—and just in time, too, because the ball came rolling right at their feet. Tim trapped it and tossed it back to Dick. Dick handed it to Elijah, who inbounded it to Mike. Dick started to follow the action, but before he took off, he called out to Tim.

"Find me after dinner tonight," he said. "I want to talk to you about something."

"Uh, sure," Tim replied. Then the play moved on, and Dick with it.

Jordan shot him a look of admiration. "Wow, you're pretty tight with Dick Dunbar, huh?"

Tim shrugged nonchalantly, although now his insides were glowing with pride. That glow faded a moment later, however, as he began to wonder what Dick wanted to talk to him about. It faded completely when he realized it could only be about one thing: his lousy jump shot!

Dick had spent a lot of time helping him with his jumper last summer. How must he have felt when Tim's first attempt was so soundly rejected?

I'll just have to prove to him that I'm a better shot, that's all, Tim thought. He hoped he'd get the chance—and if he did, that he'd have the guts to take it.

The pickup game between the shirts and the skins ended half an hour later with a narrow victory by Tito's team. Tim got back into the game and made a few points. None were off of jump shots, however. Whenever the opportunity came, he choked or simply passed the ball.

Mike quickly picked up on his reluctance to shoot from outside. Now whenever Tim had the ball beyond the key, Mike left him alone instead of covering him closely. He couldn't have made it any plainer that he didn't consider Tim a shooting threat.

After the game, everyone headed back to the Eagles Nest, showered, and then walked to the dining hall together for dinner. Tim saw Billy at a table with a group of boys he didn't know. Other waterfront campers, he figured. Billy beckoned for Tim to join them, but Tim indicated that he'd stick with the basketball players. Billy shrugged and then leaned in to listen to something one of his tablemates was saying.

Guess I don't have to worry about him making friends this year, Tim thought as he loaded his plate with chicken and potatoes.

He ate quickly and quietly, and when he was done, he cleared his dishes and set out to meet Dick.

He found him sitting at the table back at the cabin.

"Ah, right on time," Dick said. He pushed back an empty chair with his foot. "Have a seat."

Tim did. "So, um, about my jump shot—" he began.

Dick held up a hand. "Yeah, it wasn't falling for you today, was it?" he said. "Although you have to take them for them to fall, I guess. Why didn't you shoot more? Mike was giving you plenty of space."

Tim sighed heavily. "When Mike blocked me so easily…I dunno, I guess I just lost confidence in myself or something. It was different when I was at home," he hurried to add. "I made a lot of outside shots during games."

"Then what's the trouble here?" Dick wanted to know.

Tim put his head on the table and groaned. "Gruber, that's the trouble. I let him get to me all the time! I'm an idiot!"

Dick chuckled. "Hey, don't beat yourself up about it! You've honed your mechanics in the past year. Now you just have to trust your shot and put it to use—no matter who's defending you. Once you can do that, you'll be unstoppable."

Then he paused and tapped a finger on the table. "Of course, there is another shot that might make you even more unstoppable. Not everyone can do it, but I have a hunch you could learn."

Tim looked up hopefully. "What is it? Can you teach me now?"

But Dick shook his head. "Not tonight," he said. "There's something else I want to talk to you about." He picked up a sheet of paper. "I have a big problem, and I hope you can help me."

21

4

Tim blinked. Dick Dunbar, college star, potential number-one draft pick, and probable future NBA great, needed *his* help? Had the world turned upside down when he wasn't looking?

His expression must have revealed his amazement because Dick laughed to himself. "I'm in charge of a new mentoring program this summer," he explained. "Maybe you read about it in the camp brochures?"

Tim thought for a moment. "Is that the thing where younger campers learn stuff from older campers?"

Dick nodded. "Two mentors from the

Eagles Nest had signed up. One of them was Derek Chang."

"Derek? I don't think I've seen him yet."

"And you won't," Dick said, "because he broke his leg yesterday and had to drop out of camp altogether. That leaves three seven-year-olds without a mentor unless..." He raised his eyebrows, waiting for Tim to connect the dots.

"Me?" Tim squeaked. "You want *me* to be a mentor to a bunch of seven-year-olds?" He shook his head. "I don't know, Dick. The only experience I have with little kids is my bratty sister, Tara. I've never babysat anyone before."

"It's not babysitting," Dick objected. "You teach the kids basic basketball skills, then lead them through a demonstration on Parent Pickup Day."

"So I'd be a coach?"

Dick waggled his head from side to side. "Sort of, but there's more to it. A mentor takes his mentees under his wing, really gets to know them, on and off the court. Teaching is a big part of it, though."

Tim shifted in his seat. "Say they don't learn anything from me? What then?"

Dick considered the question. "Have you ever been on a team with someone who didn't like to play basketball?"

Tim immediately thought of Billy. "Yeah. Every time he was on the court, he wanted to be somewhere else."

"Try to keep that in mind when you're working with the kids," Dick suggested. "Show them how much fun playing basketball can be. If they enjoy what they're doing, they'll want to continue doing it, and then I guarantee they'll learn something—even if it's just how to dribble without hitting their own feet! And don't worry, you'll still have plenty of time to work on your own skills, because the commitment is just an hour or two a day." He smiled. "And here's the best part:

24

You have my permission to skip arts and crafts to do the program."

Tim had to laugh at that. Of all the camp activities, spending time in the arts and crafts center was his least favorite—as Dick apparently knew!

"Okay," he said at last. "I'll do it. But Dick—why me?"

Dick's smile broadened. "Truthfully?" he said, standing up. "I hadn't thought of asking you until this afternoon. Then I saw how you went out of your way to welcome Jordan, Sam, and Elijah. If you treat Red, Peter, and Keanu the same way, you'll do great."

He handed Tim some paperwork about the program, including suggestions for simple drills and ways to deal with young children. He told Tim to read through it and then headed for his room.

"Come to the outdoor courts tomorrow after breakfast," he called just before he closed his door. "You and the other mentor will meet your kids then. And thanks again, Tim. You're really doing me a big favor."

Tim waved and then set off for his own room. He was halfway there when he heard footsteps and laughter outside the front door of the cabin. Tim thought about waiting for the boys, but then he heard Mike Gruber's voice.

"Did you see his expression when I jammed him?" Mike boasted. "He was so terrified he didn't shoot again all game!"

Tim felt his face turn red. He hurried the rest of the way to his room, closing his door with a soft click. He settled down on his bunk to read through the papers Dick had given him. It had been a long day, though; the next thing he knew, it was morning, and Billy was calling his name.

"Hey, Tim, you plan to sleep in your clothes every night?" Billy asked from the other bunk.

Tim yawned. "Nah, it's a onetime thing."

26

He told him about the mentoring program as he got dressed.

"Huh, sounds pretty cool," Billy said. "So who's the other mentor from the Nest?"

"I forgot to ask," Tim confessed. "Gotta be someone decent, though, right?"

"I don't know about that," Billy replied. "After all, you're doing it!" He ducked out the door before the pillow Tim threw hit him in the face.

As Tim finished dressing, he went through the list of Eagles Nest campers, trying to guess who might be the other mentor. Donnie would be great with little kids, he bet. Cue Ball's jokes would keep everyone laughing. Or maybe Bobby Last?

But of all the possibilities, the person he saw standing with Dick at the courts after breakfast that morning was the last one he would have picked!

Gruber! Are you kidding me? Tim thought with dismay. Every fiber in his body screamed for him to run in the opposite direction. But he didn't. Dick was counting on him, and he wasn't about to let him down, Mike Gruber or no Mike Gruber.

Mike didn't look all that pleased to see him, either. "Too bad Derek broke his leg," he said. Maybe Mike really felt sorry for Derek, but Tim guessed there was a second, unspoken part to the comment: "Too bad Derek broke his leg—because now I'm stuck with you!"

Dick cleared his throat. "You guys have two options for how to work with your kids. One,

28

you can stick together and teach them in one big group. Or two, you can each take three and work with them separately."

"Separately," Tim and Mike answered immediately and in unison.

"Well, so long as you're sure," Dick said dryly. "Now help me lower the hoops a few feet."

"Lower the hoops? Why?" Mike asked.

"These guys are a lot smaller than you," Dick reminded him. "They won't be able to reach the rim if we don't drop it down." He moved to the farthest hoop.

Mike shot Tim a sideways glance and smirked. "Maybe you'll be able to hit a few now yourself, huh, shrimp?" he taunted as he headed to another basket.

Tim was fishing for a retort to fling back when Dick called, "Heads up! Here they come."

Six little boys walked toward them with a counselor. Introductions were made all around, and then the counselor left with a promise to return in an hour. Mike immediately took his three mentees to the far court. Dick departed soon after, leaving Tim alone with his three kids—and wishing he hadn't fallen asleep before reading the papers Dick had given him. Maybe there was something in them that would have given him a clue on how to begin!

"Uh, okay," Tim said. "So which one of you guys is Red?"

The smallest of the boys lifted his cap, exposing a thatch of bright orange hair.

"Oh, right," Tim said. He was a redhead, too, but his hair color was more copper than carrot. "And who's Peter?"

A chubby boy with glasses raised his hand.

"That means you're Keanu, right?" Tim said to the third boy, who, to his consternation, began flapping his arms.

"I can fly," Keanu cried, "because I have superpowers! Zoom!"

Tim was trying to figure out what to say to that when a loud voice from the other end of the court interrupted his thoughts.

"When I'm talking," Mike was saying, "I expect you to listen! Not bounce balls! Not poke each other! You got it? Good! Now *sit down.*"

The boys sat down, and Mike began describing a drill they were going to do. Tim eavesdropped for a moment. Mike sounded well prepared for the mentoring duties. And no wonder—he'd signed up for the program weeks ago, while Tim had been drafted for it just the night before.

He racked his brain, trying to come up with something—anything—to get the boys moving. He arrived at the simplest idea.

"Okay," he boomed, "three laps around the court! And no slacking!"

The three little boys looked at one another and then set off at a trot. But by the end of the second lap, they were all gasping so hard that Tim was afraid they'd pass out. So he told them to stop.

"It's so hot!" Red whined as he collapsed onto the grass. "I'm going to burst into flames!"

"I'm hungry," added Peter. "Isn't it time for lunch yet?"

Keanu was the only one who kept running. But as far as Tim could tell, he was back to pretending to be a superhero.

Tim glanced toward the other end of the court. Mike's kids were busy passing the ball back and forth, but Mike wasn't watching them. He was watching Tim—and laughing.

Tim's face reddened. Then he turned to his boys. "Enough," he said harshly. "You've got one lap left. *Move it.*" He stabbed a finger at them and then at the court.

Red shrank back. Peter's bottom lip trembled slightly. Keanu stopped in mid-zoom, his expression crestfallen. Then, one by one, they started jogging.

That's better, Tim thought, hands on hips. *Got to show them who's boss around here.*

Yet as he followed their progress around the court, Dick's suggestion to show them that basketball was fun came back to him.

Okay, so they're not having fun now, he thought. *That doesn't mean I can't make it fun!* He scratched his head, trying to figure out exactly how he could make drills enjoyable for seven-year-old boys.

It was a question he didn't find an answer to, at least not in the next hour. Those sixty minutes proved to be the longest in Tim's life. Dribbling, passing, shooting—the boys did everything he told them to do. But they performed each task with so little enthusiasm that Tim felt like he was punishing them. He didn't know who was more relieved when their counselor reappeared, him or them.

"Good job, guys," he said. He wasn't really expecting a reply—but it still hurt when he didn't get one.

6

Tim returned to the courts that afternoon
for basketball practice with the other boys
from the Eagles Nest. As he ran his warm-
up laps with the sun beating down on him, he
found himself sympathizing with Red's complaint about the heat.

*Too bad I can't turn off the sun and turn on
the cool,* he thought, *for me and for Red!*

After the laps, the players divided into two
groups, guards in one, forwards and centers
in the other. Tim was in Tito's group with
Mike, Sam, and Elijah.

"We're working on dribbling first, then outside shooting today," Tito informed them as

he placed sets of orange cones in two rows. He tossed them each a ball. "As guards, you have to be able to dribble with either hand, not just your dominant one. Let's see what you can do."

He told them to form two lines at center court. "Dribble down to the hoop and back through the cones. Speed and control the whole way. Whenever I blow my whistle, switch hands. Ready? Go!"

Tim was first in his line. At Tito's command, he took off. He focused on keeping his dribble low, using his fingertips and wrist to move the ball—and not letting Mike, who was weaving through the other cones, get ahead of him. He succeeded at all three.

Fweet! shrieked the whistle.

Without missing a beat, Tim bounced the ball to his left hand. He'd only gone a few steps when—*fweet!*—Tito blew his whistle again. Again, Tim switched hands smoothly.

Then, as he was turning around at the

baseline, Tito gave another blast. Still turning, Tim fumbled the cross dribble. The ball hit a cone and rolled off the court. Red-faced, he dodged past Mike to retrieve it.

"Watch it!" Mike growled.

Tim's face was still burning when he passed the ball to Sam, who was next in line. When all the boys had gone through the cones three times, Tito called them back together.

"A few mistakes, but overall, pretty good," Tito said. "There are plenty of drills to make your dribble even stronger. The figure eight, for example."

He got into a low stance with one leg forward. Dribbling just a few inches off the ground, he moved the ball in a half circle around his front foot, passed it between his legs to his other hand, and then dribbled it around the outside of his back foot before passing between his legs again. When complete, the ball's path formed a figure eight.

Tim had done the figure eight before, so he

didn't have any trouble with it. Mike didn't, either, but Sam and Elijah needed some practice to get it right. When they succeeded, Tito moved on to the scissor dribble.

With his feet shoulder-width apart and his right leg forward, he dribbled a few times and then bounced the ball between his legs. He caught it with his other hand and dribbled it to the front before sending between his legs again. He brought the ball even with his front leg and began the drill from the top.

"Join in," he called.

Once everyone had a good rhythm going, he urged them to increase their speed. They kept at it for a full minute before he told them to stop.

"How are your wrists and arms feeling?" he asked.

"A little tired," Elijah admitted. Tim and Sam nodded in agreement.

"Whenever you get a chance, dribble against a wall," Tito suggested. "Keeping the ball from falling will really build up your arm strength and stamina."

Tim had never heard of doing such a thing but decided it was worth a try.

"Okay, one last activity," Tito said. "Get a second ball and spread out along the center-court line." When the boys were in position, Tito told them to begin dribbling both balls, one with each hand.

"Keep them in sync until you reach the foul line," he added. "Then alternate them so one is hitting the ground while the other is hitting your hand. Turn at the baseline and come back."

The drill was harder than it sounded.

"Stay low!" Tito barked. "Eyes up, not on the ball! Control the dribbles!"

Tim was breathing hard when Tito ended the double dribble drill and sent them to Jody to work on their shooting.

"At yesterday's game," the counselor said, "Dick and I noticed that some of you didn't take shots from outside the key, even when you were wide open."

Mike suddenly coughed "Tim!" into his hand. Jody frowned. Mike thumped his chest, cleared his throat a few times, and then nodded as if to say everything was fine.

"An-y-way," Jody continued, "pair off, one person on offense, the other on defense. Offense, dribble around, throw a few fakes, and then try for a shot. Defense, be annoying but don't interfere too much. The point is to let your partner get comfortable taking shots while being guarded, not to block his every attempt."

Tim paired up with Sam and started on offense. Sam followed Jody's instructions to the letter, allowing Tim to get off several shots. Some of them missed the basket, but others banked in softly. After a few minutes, they changed sides, and Sam had his turn to drop some through the hoop.

Then Jody had them switch partners. Now

Tim faced Mike. Dread bubbled up inside him. He wondered how long it would take for Mike to make him feel foolish.

Not long, it turned out. On his first possession, Tim fake-pumped, hoping Mike would jump to block the ball, thus giving him a chance to go back up for the real shot.

But he never got that shot off, because Mike punched the ball out of his hands in mid-fake!

"Jeez, Daniels, hit the weight room already, will you?" Mike said in a mocking tone. "You're so weak you can't even hold the ball above your head!"

7

Tim was so angry he saw red before his eyes. He started toward Mike, hands balled into fists. But before he'd taken two steps, someone pulled him back. He spun around and found himself staring at Dick Dunbar.

"Is there a problem here?" Dick asked quietly.

Tim bit his lip. He wanted to tell Dick what Mike had done but realized he'd sound like a crybaby if he did. So instead, he shook his head and mumbled, "Just going to get the ball."

When he returned to the court, Dick

beckoned him over to an empty court. He called Sam over, too.

"Mike and Elijah are going to work with Jody, and I'll work with you two," he said. "You've done some one-on-one shooting, right? Let's move on to two-on-one. You two bring the ball down, work it around the key, and try for a shot. I'll play defense and try to stop you. Okay?"

Anything to get me away from Mike, Tim felt like replying. But he just nodded and moved to the center line with Sam.

Sam had the ball first. He took a few dribbles and passed to Tim. Dick leaped forward and covered him. Tim dribbled to his right. Dick matched him step for step. Tim tried to shake him off by speeding up, then stopping quickly, bouncing the ball between his legs, picking it up on his other side, and then changing direction.

Dick wasn't fooled, though, so Tim sent the ball to Sam. Sam was in good shooting position, so he turned and lofted the ball toward the hoop. It touched the backboard and dropped through the net.

"Well done!" Dick praised. "Go again."

Tim and Sam hustled back to center court. Before they began, Tim whispered, "How about the ol' give-and-go?"

Sam nodded. "I shot last time, so this time, give it to me, and then go so I can give it back!"

Tim flashed him a thumbs-up, and the two started downcourt with Tim in control of the ball. Dick came out to challenge. Tim bounced the ball to Sam, assuming that Dick would follow the ball and give him an open lane to the hoop. All Sam had to do was pass back to him and—*bloop!*—Tim would put in an easy layup.

Unfortunately, Dick didn't do what Tim expected him to. As Tim charged forward, Dick fell back to protect the basket. Tim barreled into him at full speed, waist high—and knocked the lanky center's legs right out from under him!

Dick crash-landed on his side. He rolled over with a groan, cradling his elbow, as Jody, Tito, and the Eagles rushed over. Tim backed away, his eyes wide with horror.

"Can you straighten your arm?" Jody asked.

Dick tried but only moved it a little before grimacing and shaking his head. "I think I better go to the infirmary," he said, his voice tight with pain. He looked around and found Tim. "Daniels, can you lend me a hand getting there?"

Jody frowned. "I think Tito or I should—"

"Tim got hit hard, too," Dick interjected. "I want him to get checked out."

Jody helped him to his feet. "He's all yours, Tim. Make sure he gets there in one piece."

Tim nodded dumbly. Then he and Dick headed to the infirmary. It was slow going and silent except for the occasional grunt of pain from Dick. They had almost reached their destination when Dick paused.

"I don't really think you're hurt," he said. "I wanted you to come with me so I could tell you I don't blame you for what happened. It was an accident. Basketball is a contact sport, no matter what anyone tells you. I've been injured before—and a lot worse than this!"

"But what if it's really bad?" Tim whispered. "Like, bad enough to end your career before it's even begun?"

Dick laid the hand of his uninjured arm on Tim's shoulder. "Remember what I said about not putting all my eggs in one basket? I've got backup plans if basketball doesn't work out. If this injury is bad enough to keep me off the court forever—and I really don't think it is—then I've got plenty of other options."

He pointed a finger at Tim. "So now that you know that, I hereby order you *not* to beat yourself up over this. Deal?"

"Deal," Tim agreed.

They mounted the steps of the infirmary together. As Tim pushed open the door, Dick smiled at him. "By the way, I don't know where Gruber gets off calling you weak. You hit me like a linebacker going for the quarterback!"

Tim left Dick with the nurse on duty. He wanted to stick around, but the nurse told him that it was getting close to dinner and that he needed to return to his camp unit or else he'd miss eating that night. It had been a busy day and Tim was hungry, so he did as the nurse instructed. Besides, Dick told him to go.

Campers were pouring into the dining hall, talking and laughing as usual. Tim joined the food line. He picked up his tray and reached for his silverware. His fork, still hot from the dishwasher, burned his fingers.

"Ouch!" He dropped it with a loud clatter and waved his hand through the air to cool it.

46

That's when he noticed that a strange silence had fallen around him. He looked around to see what was going on—and gulped.

Everyone around him was staring at him. One camper nudged another. "That's the guy who took out Dick Dunbar."

Like a flash, word of what had happened spread like wildfire throughout the dining hall. Soon, every person at camp knew that a kid named Tim Daniels had injured basketball star Dick Dunbar.

It didn't matter that Dick didn't blame Tim. Everyone else at Camp Wickasaukee did.

The next day was the worst of Tim's life. Most of the Eagles shunned him—the only exceptions were Billy and Sam. Their efforts to cheer him up might have worked if Tim hadn't heard a rumor that Dick needed an operation to fix his arm.

The morning mentor session was disastrous. Tim yelled himself hoarse trying to get Red, Peter, and Keanu to pay attention to his instructions.

The afternoon practice was equally awful. Without Dick around, the Eagles turned in a lackluster performance on the court. Even Tito and Jody, usually so full of competitive energy, appeared not to care how their players executed their drills.

And that was a problem, for the first of three inter-camp matches was scheduled for the next day. The basketball game between the Eagles Nest and Camp Woodbine's thirteen- and fourteen-year-old boys was the last competition of that match. If Wickasaukee and Woodbine were close in points by the day's end, that game would decide which camp was the overall winner. So the Eagles needed to be fired up and fully prepared.

But the players couldn't seem to pull it together. They blamed one another for mistakes, loudly pointed out one another's faults, and ran their plays so haphazardly that few of them worked. Tito became so aggravated that he kicked a basketball into a nearby field. Jody's frown deepened with each passing minute until he looked like a volcano ready to explode.

"We're going to get crushed tomorrow,"

Tim told Billy when they met up in their room before dinner.

Truer words had never been spoken. While Camp Wickasaukee emerged victorious at the end of the day of events, it was no thanks to the Eagles. They lost their match 62–47.

Tim had spent most of the last quarter of the game on the bench, watching Mike Gruber try to single-handedly erase the point deficit. Whenever Tim did get in, it was as if he didn't exist. Except for inbounding passes to Elijah, he barely touched the ball because no one passed to him.

Not that it mattered, he thought. *I probably would have botched the play or tossed up an air ball anyway.*

Despite the basketball players' dismal showing, the mood in the Eagles Nest before dinner was celebratory. Several of the non-basketball players had performed well in their events.

Billy had been the top swimmer of both

camps, Tim found out later. He congratulated his friend enthusiastically. But in the next breath, he began to pour out his frustration at how the game had gone.

Billy stopped him after a moment. "Why don't you talk to Dick about all this stuff? He might be able to help you better than me."

Tim glared at him from his bunk. Some friend he was; after Tim had put up with Billy's complaints all last summer, Billy couldn't even listen to one of his!

"How am I supposed to talk to Dick?" he snapped. "He's still in the hospital!"

"No, he's not," Billy retorted. "He's in the infirmary."

Tim sat bolt upright. "What? Since when?"

"Since an hour ago," Billy said. "I heard some of the waterfront guys talking about it."

Tim leaped to his feet and raced out the door.

"No need to thank me!" Billy called after him.

Tim took off at a run for the infirmary, his mind racing. *How serious is Dick's injury? Will he be sidelined for a few days or the rest of the summer, or*—Tim gulped—*will it mean the end of his career?*

He bounded up the steps of the infirmary two at a time and burst through the door.

"Goodness, young man, what's the problem? Is someone hurt?" the nurse on duty asked in alarm.

"No! I'm looking for Dick Dunbar!" Tim gasped.

"You found him."

Tim spun around to see Dick reclining in a hospital bed. His eyes widened as he took in the cast on Dick's arm. "Oh, man," he groaned. "How bad is it?"

To his relief, Dick laughed. "I told you, I've had worse."

He shook his head when Tim asked about the operation. "Is that the rumor going around the camp? Don't worry. I didn't have an operation. It was a clean break, and a pretty minor one, too, from what I saw on the X-ray. I was about to check out of here, in fact. You can carry my bag. Come on."

Tim soon had Dick settled in a chair in his room.

"That's better," Dick said with a sigh. "Now tell me: How are things going with you?"

Tim hesitated. He wanted to tell Dick how everything—from his mentoring sessions to his playing to his relationships with the other Eagles—was falling apart. But he was ashamed to admit that he was having so many problems.

Then Dick looked him straight in the eye and said, "Come on. Out with it. *All* of it."

So Tim launched into a review of the past two days. Dick listened attentively until Tim hung his head and wondered aloud if he should just pack up and go home. "Nobody wants me here anyway. Not my mentees, not my teammates, and maybe not even Billy."

"Funny," Dick said then, "I didn't peg you for a quitter. Last year, when your shot wasn't falling, when Mike and the other boys were giving you grief, when Billy needed a boost, you didn't run and hide. You found solutions!"

He ticked off his fingers one by one. "You got my help with your shot. You turned the tables on the practical jokers. You handed Billy the biggest shot of the summer—and when he made it, you turned him into a hero, at least for the day. So my question to you is: Why are you shying away from these new challenges?"

"I don't know." Tim looked up. "You ever feel overwhelmed by stuff?"

"Sometimes," Dick admitted.

"What do you do about it?"

Dick thought for a moment before answering. "You ever eat a whole pizza by yourself?"

Tim frowned. "Yeah, but what does that—"

"Did you eat it all at once or one slice at a time?" Dick pressed.

"A slice at a time."

Dick sat back with a satisfied smile. "Exactly!"

Tim stared at Dick, completely baffled. Then, slowly, he figured out what Dick was trying to say.

"My problems are like the pizza, right?" he ventured. "I can't tackle them all at once any more than I can eat a whole pizza in one bite. But if I take the problems one at a time — like slices of pizza — I might be able to deal with them."

"And the first problem you're going to take care of," Dick said, rising clumsily out of his chair, "is your shooting trouble. I haven't forgotten about my promise to teach you a shot that could help." He stopped at the door and looked over his shoulder. "Well? You coming or not?"

With hope rising in his chest, Tim jumped up. "You bet I am!"

9

Dick led Tim to the indoor gymnasium. He produced a key, unlocked a side entrance, and ushered Tim inside.

The gym was empty. Patches of late afternoon sun gleamed on the shiny wooden floor, dust swirling in the beams. Their footsteps echoed and squeaked as they moved to the bleachers.

"Wow, this place is so different when there's no one here!" The cavernous space amplified Tim's voice so that it sounded as if he'd yelled rather than whispered. "Is it okay for us to be here?"

Dick waved away his concern. "You're here

with me, so it's fine," he said. "Now, as to why we're here. You ever heard of a hook shot?"

"Sure," Tim responded. "Lots of NBA players use it. Kareem Abdul-Jabbar of the Lakers was the master. Magic Johnson learned from him. Nowadays, Tim Duncan is—holy cow!" His eyes widened. "Is *that* the shot you're going to teach me?"

Dick laughed. "That's the one. Even though I can't demonstrate it," he added with a gesture toward his cast, "I can talk you through it. Head to the upper-right corner of the key."

"Should I take a ball?"

Dick shook his head. "I want you to practice the motions first."

He continued talking while Tim went to the key. "The hook shot gets its name because the shooter's arm hooks over his head during the shot. But that's just a small part of the whole move. Proper footwork, body position, and well-timed release of the ball are equally crucial to getting the shot to fall.

"The hook shot is difficult to block," Dick went on, "because the shooter's body stays between the ball and the defender. The beauty of the shot is that you can do it any time the defense is covering you tightly. And, if for some reason you decide not to send it toward the hoop, you can convert it into a pass to an open player instead. But for now, practice it as a shot."

He instructed Tim to turn so his left shoulder was aimed at the hoop. "The next steps happen all at the same time, but we'll go through them one by one."

"Like slices of pizza?" Tim said with a smile.

"Pepperoni pizza, to be exact," Dick replied. "First, the ball. Pretend you're holding one in your right hand. Now bring it up in an arc from low to high until your elbow is about shoulder height and the ball is above your head."

He and Tim went through the motion together. "Obviously," Dick said, "you'll be moving a lot faster, so the momentum will keep the ball stuck in your hand. When the ball reaches the top of the arc, flick your wrist and shoot."

Tim pretended to shoot.

"Good," Dick praised. "Now for another part. The ball's in your right hand. So use your left arm as a barrier, like you're protecting your dribble."

"Like this?" Tim raised his left arm so it was nearly parallel with the floor. He made sure his elbow was jutting out, ready to defend against an attack.

"Yes. You look at any picture of Kareem as he flicks in the hook, you'll see his non-shooting arm in a position like that," Dick said. "Now the footwork. Your left foot is your pivot foot and so stays nailed to the floor. As the ball reaches the top of the arc, push off and straight up with your right foot. That way, you'll be at the

greatest-possible height just when you're re-
leasing the ball."

Tim made a face. "What are the chances
my 'greatest-possible height' will be high
enough to get the ball over Mike Gruber's
hands?" he asked.

Dick smiled. "If you do the move right,
your chances are very good. Imagine a line
drawn from your left elbow to the upraised
ball. It goes up an angle, right? So to reach
the ball, Mike, or whoever is defending you,
wouldn't just have to jump up—he'd have to
jump on top of you!" He shrugged. "Sure, he
might get the ball, but he'd foul you in the
process. Might even get called for a technical
because it'd be a pretty flagrant foul. Now,
let's see you go through the whole motion a
few times."

Tim took a moment to picture what he was
supposed to do and then shot five pretend
hooks.

"Not bad!" Dick said. He picked up a basketball and tossed it to Tim. "Now with the ball. Aim for the hoop."

Tim's first few attempts flew wide of their mark.

"Eyes on the hoop, not your hands!" Dick corrected.

Tim nodded. The next attempts hit the backboard but didn't go in. Then, on his seventh try, the basketball kissed the glass and swished softly through the net's strings.

"I did it!" Tim cried. He hurried to retrieve the ball, set up for the shot again—and sank it!

"Two in a row!" he crowed happily.

Two became three, but his fourth one missed. Dick instructed him to try the same shot but with his other hand and from the other corner of the key. Tim was right-handed, so most of these attempts were way off. He didn't mind, however. He knew it would take a lot of practice to get the shot to fall consistently, no matter where he was standing or which hand he was using. But he was going to keep trying because if Dick was right, he'd finally have something that would work against Mike Gruber!

"I'm feeling really good about this shot," he said to Dick.

"You should," Dick replied. "Of course, you'll feel even better about it when you know you can hit it during practice or, better yet, a game."

Tim's face fell. "Oh, man, that's right! I've got to practice it when someone's defending me. But who's going to help me with that? I'll tell you who—no one!"

10

The hook shot lesson came to an end a few minutes later because dinner was starting. Tim and Dick walked together into the dining hall, where Dick was immediately surrounded by people asking about his injury.

Tim moved away to pick up his food. He sat down at an empty table to eat, chewing slowly as he thought about his newest predicament.

The hook shot promised to be a very powerful tool. But the shot was worthless unless it worked during a game. And the only way to make it work during a game was to practice it in gamelike situations. To do that, he needed a defender.

Dick would have been his first choice, but obviously, he was out.

Then who? Tim glanced at the table where the other boys from the Eagles Nest had gathered. *Sam? He's been friendly, even when everyone else was ignoring me.*

Even as the thought crossed Tim's mind, Sam said something that made Mike Gruber laugh uproariously. Tim shook his head. Sam was friendly—with everyone. If he helped Tim, would he be able to keep the practice sessions a secret from the others? Tim wasn't sure.

That was the trouble, Tim realized. He needed someone who knew how to play basketball well enough to defend against him. But if he was to keep his new weapon a secret from Mike, it would be best if that person wasn't on the Eagles Nest team.

Who do I know who fits that description?

He finished his supper without coming up with the answer. He was on his way out the door when someone called his name.

"Hey, Tim! Wait up!"

Tim turned to see Billy hurrying toward him. "Hi, Billy, how's it—" He stopped in mid-sentence and clapped his hand to his forehead. "*Billy!* Of course! Why didn't I think of you before?"

Billy gave Tim a wary look. "Think of me before what?"

Tim pulled Billy away from the other campers who were leaving the dining hall and explained the situation to his friend. "So I was hoping that while everyone else is at the bonfire tonight, you could help me practice the shot. What do you say?"

Billy chewed on his lower lip. "Won't we get in trouble for skipping the fire without permission?"

"We won't miss the whole thing," Tim assured him. "We'll show up at the start. Then we'll ask to use the latrine or something. We'll practice for half an hour and then come back before anyone misses us. Come on, please?"

Billy let out a long sigh. "Fine," he said. "If it's that important to you, I'll do it. But if we get caught—"

"I'll take full blame," Tim promised.

An hour later, Tim and Billy were at the bonfire with the rest of the Eagles Nest. They were singing along to a ridiculous song about a dog named Lima who had roamed away from home only to return "all nice and clean," prompting the question, "Where, oh where, has Lima been?" The song went on and on, with campers shouting out the names of different beans like coffee, string, and jelly.

While the other boys were laughing and singing, Tim poked Billy and whispered, "Let's go!"

Billy looked nervous, but he followed Tim into the darkness. They found the paved path that led to the outdoor courts. But before they got there, Tim heard the sound of girls laughing and basketballs bouncing on the hardtop. Members of the girls' camp were already there.

"Change of plans!" he hissed to Billy. "This way!" He veered onto a new path with Billy at his heels.

But when Billy saw where they were headed, he stopped short. "The gym? Are you nuts? We're not allowed in there!"

Tim knew Billy was right. But he was so desperate to practice the hook shot that he refused to give up. So when Billy started to leave, Tim caught hold of his shirt and tugged him back.

"Let's just check the door," he said persuasively. "If it's locked, we leave. If not, we'll get in a little bit of practice and then leave."

They stared at each other for a long minute. Then Billy rolled his eyes. "I don't know how I let you talk me into these things."

Tim hadn't really expected the door to be open, but the handle twisted easily in his grip. He pushed the door open and stepped inside.

If the empty gym had seemed weird in the afternoon, at night it was downright eerie. Pale moonbeams cast ghostly shadows. The basket strings hung like giant spiderwebs in the gloom; all that was missing, Tim thought with a shiver, were multi-eyed, eight-legged monsters. Even the bleachers looked frightening, rising up the side walls like black, jagged cliffs. Anyone—or anything—could be lurking there!

Billy shrank back and would have bolted if Tim hadn't grabbed his arm. Tim started to whisper that they'd only stay for half an hour. Then he heard a small sound. He turned to see what it was—and the words died in his throat.

A closet door was slowly creaking open. As he stared, a ghastly head rose out of the shadows!

11

Billy let out a squeak of terror, pulled free of Tim's grasp, lurched sideways into the doorway, and fled. Tim wanted to follow but couldn't make his feet or legs work.

Then suddenly, the gymnasium flooded with light.

"Who's there?"

A girl stepped through the doorway underneath the horrifying apparition. Tim was about to cry out a warning when he saw that the girl was holding a stick—and that the stick was attached to the ghost!

That's when he recognized the ghost for

what it really was: a very creepy papier-mâché clown puppet, complete with exaggerated smile, bulbous nose, and wide, staring eyes. Last year, the puppet had lived at the arts and crafts center. Tim would never admit it, but its presence was the main reason he'd disliked the place.

He recognized the girl then, too. "Wanda? Is that you?"

The girl blinked in surprise and then smiled. "Tim! Long time no see!"

Tim had met Wanda the summer before. Then, she'd had a mouth full of braces and been short and stocky. The braces were gone now, and although she only came up to Tim's shoulders, she was slimmer. Her smile was just as warm and friendly as ever.

"What are you doing with that?" Tim asked, pointing to the clown head.

Wanda made a face. "Kim, my counselor, made me come get it. She wants to stick it in the latrines as a joke." She shuddered. "Can

70

you imagine opening the stall door and seeing this?"

Tim pulled back in mock horror. "As if the latrines weren't bad enough already!" They laughed together.

"So now you know why I'm here," Wanda said, leaning the clown head against the door frame. "How about you?"

Tim decided there was no harm in telling Wanda the truth.

"Hook shot, huh?" she said when he was finished. "That'll be one tasty move to get under your belt."

"Yeah, too bad I can't work on it tonight," Tim said. "My defender ran away when he saw ol' clown face."

Wanda tucked a stray lock of hair behind her ear. "I could help you," she offered.

Tim considered accepting. Then he thought about how he'd feel if Wanda got in trouble because of him. So he shook his head.

"Thanks, but I don't think so. Not because

you're a girl!" he added hurriedly when Wanda frowned. "I don't have permission to be here. If I get caught—"

"I have permission," Wanda interrupted. "If anyone comes by, I'll just say you were helping me find the clown."

When Tim still hesitated, she put her hands on her hips. "What? Don't think I'm good enough?"

"I'm sure you're a great basketball player," Tim hastened to say. "But I really need to practice with someone a little, you know"—he gestured helplessly—"*taller.*" He hoped she wasn't as sensitive about her height as he was about his.

To his relief, she burst out laughing. "Yeah, too bad I can't grow a foot in the next minute! Although," she added, "I could grow a head taller!"

She picked up the clown and held the stick so that the head was eyeball to eyeball with Tim. "How you like me now?" she growled, shaking the puppet and making a length of cloth attached to the clown's neck flutter.

Tim chuckled. "Okay! I guess any practice is better than none—even though it means facing *that!*"

He found a basketball, and they moved to center court. Wanda got into the best stance she could while holding the puppet stick. Tim dribbled toward the three-point line. Wanda matched him step for step. The puppet actually did make her seem much bigger and taller; Tim held out his left arm to protect the ball, even though she couldn't possibly go for a steal.

He reached the top corner of the key and set himself for the hook shot. Wanda stuck close to him, bobbing the puppet around in an imitation of a real defender. Tim tried to ignore it as he swept the ball up from his hip and sent it over the clown's head and toward the hoop with a flick of his wrist. He landed, mentally crossing his fingers that the shot would hit its mark.

It hit, all right, but a spot high on the backboard instead of close to the hoop. It ricocheted off at an angle and landed on the opposite side of the court.

Tim shook his head in disgust and retrieved the ball. On his second attempt, the ball struck the front of the rim and bounced off. But the third time he took the hook, it flew in a perfect half circle before swishing cleanly through the strings.

"Yes!" Tim cried, jabbing a finger at the clown. "In your face, Gruber!"

Wanda laughed. "Is that what we're calling it?" She studied the clown's face. "You know, I can see the resemblance! I hereby dub this creepy clown Gruber!"

"Works for me," Tim said with a grin.

"That last hook shot was working for you, too," Wanda said. She repositioned herself behind the clown. "Gruber and I are ready whenever you are!"

Tim practiced the hook shot for another

twenty minutes. He used his right hand most of the time, only shifting to his left at Wanda's suggestion. He bricked every attempt from that side. But when he started to get down on himself, Wanda made a joke or said the trouble was with Gruber the clown, not Tim.

They called it quits when Wanda realized she'd been away from her cabin for more than half an hour. They turned off the lights and went outside. She locked up the gym, bid Tim a hasty good-bye, and took off at a run. The puppet bounced above her, the cloth around its neck flying out behind it like a cape.

Seeing the cape reminded Tim of Keanu zooming around like a superhero. *Too bad capes are only used in basketball during the NBA Slam Dunk contest,* he thought as he walked back toward the Eagles Nest. *I bet Keanu would like basketball if he got to wear one during practice. I can see him now: cape around his neck, arms reaching up as he leaps to take off in flight!*

He chuckled at the image. Then suddenly, a new thought struck him. He stopped in his tracks. *Arms up as he leaps*, he mused. *That's how a defender blocks a shot. I wonder…*

12

The campfire was just ending when Tim returned. He managed to slip into the crowd unnoticed. Billy was already in their room when he reached the cabin.

"Where've you been?" Billy demanded.

Tim explained about Wanda and the clown puppet.

"If Wanda hadn't turned on the lights just then, I would have been right behind you," he added so that his friend wouldn't feel embarrassed at having fled. "That clown is beyond creepy!"

Then he told Billy about the idea the

puppet had given him. When he was done, Billy nodded thoughtfully.

"You might as well give it a try," Billy said. "If the kids go for it, great. If not"—he shrugged—"what's the worst that can happen?"

The next morning after breakfast, Tim arrived at the basketball courts carrying white sheets he'd gotten from the arts and crafts center, plus a handful of clothespins. Mike and his mentees were already hard at work at one end of the courts. When Tim saw them, he almost changed his mind about putting his new plan into action.

What's the worst that can happen? he echoed Billy's question from the previous night. *I can make a fool of myself in front of Gruber again, that's what!*

Then Keanu raced past him, arms outstretched and making zooming noises, and Tim decided he might as well try it after all.

Tim called his boys together. "We're going

to work on defensive positioning today," he told them. He expected them to groan—and he wasn't disappointed.

"We already did that," Red complained.

"Yeah, well, today we're going to do it differently. Keanu, come here." When the boy came forward, Tim pinned a sheet around his neck.

Keanu opened his eyes wide. "Cool!" he cried, twisting around to admire his new apparel.

Red and Peter jumped up and demanded capes of their own. Tim put one around each of their necks and let Red tie one around his own neck, too. Then he turned to Keanu. "Show me what a superhero looks like when he takes off to fly."

Keanu's arms snapped straight up over his head.

"Freeze!"

Keanu froze.

"This is how you should look when you're

guarding a shooter," Tim said. "When your arms are up, it's a whole lot harder for him to get the shot off. And as you know," he improvised, "superheroes have to jump to take off. So do basketball players who are defending the hoop."

He held his arms overhead and jumped as if blocking a shot. The boys imitated him. As they did, Tim noticed one of Mike's kids watching them.

Tim beckoned Red, Peter, and Keanu closer. "I think we need a secret code name for this move," he said in a low voice. "How about 'take off'? Whenever you hear it, put your arms up and jump. Okay?"

"Okay!" all three whispered conspiratorially.

"Then let's try it. Take off!"

The boys thrust their arms up high and jumped straight up as if reaching for the sky.

Tim stepped back as if amazed. "Wow! For a minute there, I thought you really were about to fly!"

The boys giggled. Then Red raised his hand. "I know another move we can do!" He got into a low crouch, gathered the ends of his cape into his hands, and held his arms out at a downward angle—the classic defender's position.

"Good!" Tim praised. "What's its code name?"

"'Shield,'" Red answered immediately, "because a superhero would hold his cape like this to shield someone behind him."

"But what if the person he was protecting was moving around?" Tim prodded.

Red thought for a minute. Then, still in his crouch and with his cape held out, he sidestepped one way and then the other.

Tim grinned broadly. "Yes! And that's just what you guys have to do whenever you're on defense. Low stance, arms wide, and sidestep—shield!"

"I've got one!" Peter said excitedly. "Remember when you said we should keep our eyes glued to our man's middle, because wherever his gut goes, he'll go?"

Tim was pleased to know that something he'd said had sunk in. "That's right. Your guy can fake you out of position with other parts of his body—his head and arms, or by stutter-stepping, for example. But it's nearly impossible to move your midsection one way while you're going another. Believe me, I've tried to do it! So what's your thought, Peter?"

Peter pointed two fingers at his eyes and then touched them to Tim's middle. " 'Laser vision'! We pretend to bore a hole right through our guy." He narrowed his eyes, stared at Tim's belly button, and made a sizzling sound with his lips.

They all laughed. Then Tim paired Peter with Keanu and Red with himself. "Let's test out our codes." He told Peter to pretend to dribble. To Keanu and Red, he said, "Shield!"

The two defenders immediately dropped into a defender's stance.

"Laser vision!"

Red stared so hard at Tim's stomach that Tim swore he could actually see smoke rising from that spot. He leaned over then and whispered something in Peter's ear. Straightening, he gave Peter a nod and said, "Ready? Go!"

Peter took off, dribbling an imaginary ball. Keanu looked startled but recovered quickly. A few rapid sidesteps put him between Peter and the basket.

"Shield," Tim heard him mutter. "Laser vision!"

And when Peter jumped as if to shoot, Keanu jumped, too, whipping his hands above his head and mouthing, "Take off!"

Red jumped up and down. "Is it our turn now?" he asked eagerly.

Tim nodded. Satisfaction spread through his body as Red followed him step for step to the hoop.

The satisfaction faded a moment later,

however. That's when he saw Mike's kids working through a complex drill sequence at the other end of the courts. Mike stood to one side, but he wasn't looking at his threesome. He was watching Tim. Even from a distance, Tim could see the scorn in his face.

Tim suddenly saw his mentees through Mike's eyes. Compared to Mike's kids, Red, Peter, and Keanu looked like guests at a superhero-themed birthday party. All that was missing was the cake and ice cream.

With that thought, he reached up to remove his cape. But a small hand stopped him. He looked down to see Keanu grinning up at him.

"This is the best practice ever!" the boy cried.

Tim stared at him. Then, with a broad smile, he tightened the knot at his throat and silently vowed not to let Mike ruin the beginning he'd made that day.

And he better watch out at practice, too!

13

Tim hit the court for the Eagles afternoon session with renewed determination. Giving up was no longer an option. Playing the best he could—and earning a slot in the starting lineup—were the only goals he had.

He sprinted his laps. He fired hard, accurate passes. He dribbled with control, switching hands with more dexterity than he even knew he had.

"You are *intense* today," Donnie DeGeronimo commented after Tim stole the ball and drove the length of the court for a layup.

"Must have been something I ate," Tim growled as he hustled back on defense.

"Well, save me a piece next time," Cue Ball put in. "I'm always hungry for stuff like that!"

Donnie and Cue Ball weren't the only ones who noticed Tim's improved playing. "You're showing me something here, Daniels," Tito called after Tim faked a shot and then bounced a pass around his defender. "I like it. I like it a lot!"

Tim acknowledged the praise but didn't let it boost his confidence too much. Only after he'd sunk a few jumpers during their scrimmage did he give himself a mental pat on the back.

None of those shots was a hook because he needed more practice first. Dick Dunbar must have realized why he wasn't shooting that particular shot because after dinner, he pressed the key to the gym into Tim's hand and told him to return it when he was through.

Tim found Billy, who was more than willing to help out once he knew they had Dick's permission to use the gym. Tim wondered if he'd run into Wanda there again, but he and Billy had the indoor court to themselves. The session went well, with Tim hitting the hook consistently despite heavy pressure from Billy.

"You sure you don't want to rejoin the team?" Tim asked his friend at one point. "You're playing really well!"

Billy shrugged. "Who knows? Maybe."

After so much basketball, Tim slept like a log that night. He woke up refreshed and ready to try out a new drill with Red, Keanu, and Peter. He'd gotten the idea after lunch the day before, when he'd seen a camper frantically licking an ice cream cone that was melting all down his hand.

"I call it dribbling without dribbling," Tim told his three boys the next morning. He led them to the camp concession stand, where he bought them each an ice cream cone. Before they started eating, he took them to the paved path and handed them each a basketball.

"Hold your cones out, like this"—he positioned his left arm away from his body and almost parallel to the ground—"and dribble the ball with your free hand. Now this is the important part: keep your eyes on your ice cream at all times! When it starts to melt, lick it. But don't stop dribbling the ball!"

As a guard, Tim knew how important it was to learn to dribble without watching the ball. He figured the best way to teach the little boys this skill was to give them something better than the ball to look at. Maybe it wasn't the usual way, but it seemed to work. The boys finished their cones quickly but continued to practice their heads-up dribble long after the last bite.

Back at the court, Tim and his mentees played hot potato so they could work on making their chest passes fast, sharp, and accurate. Then he switched the game to bounce passes, renaming the drill mashed potato just to hear them laugh. Finally, in a drill he called potato, potato, who has the potato, he put one boy in the middle with instructions to intercept the ball that he and the other two boys were passing to and fro.

"All this potato talk makes me hope they're serving french fries with lunch!" he joked.

That afternoon at the outdoor courts, Tim inched closer to a starting spot on the Eagles with his own heads-up play. Later, his night session at the indoor gym was the best yet. Not only did he sink more hook shots than ever before, but also Wanda reappeared to put Gruber the clown puppet back in the closet. Before she stowed it, however, she took Billy's place on the court and used it to help Tim practice.

"You've got to try the hook shot in the game against Camp Chickasaw," Billy urged him. "They won't be able to shut you down!"

Wanda nodded. "You've really improved since that first session. I think you could make it work for you."

"Maybe," Tim said evasively. "If I'm feeling it after tomorrow's practice...maybe."

The next morning, Tim had another fun mentoring session. This time, he took the kids to the waterfront, led them into the water above their waists, and handed them each a ball.

"We're in the water for two reasons. One, so you'll learn to start your jump shot with the ball held above, not at, your waist. Bringing the ball up from down low gives your defender extra time to slap it out of your hands. Here in the water, you'll have to start the shot high because the water is in your way."

"What's the second reason?" Red asked.

Tim splashed him. "I was getting tired of hearing you complain about the heat!"

He showed them how to grip the ball with the fingers of their shooting hand spread across the ball's stripes and the other hand holding the ball in place. "Use your finger pads, not your whole hand," he added. "Then, as you jump for the shot, push the ball

90

straight up and, at the very top, flick your wrist to send it arcing to the hoop."

Peter gave it a try. "Whoa!" he cried in astonishment when he landed. "I feel like I jumped a mile into the air!"

"That's because the water makes you buoyant," Tim said. "You've got hang time like Dwight Howard or LeBron James!"

"Hey, that should be the code word for this!" Peter said.

"What, Dwight Howard?" Tim asked. "Or LeBron James?"

"No—'hang time'!"

"I'm good with that," Tim said. "Now enough talk. Get your hang time going, boys!"

Tim watched the boys practice their shots, stepping in every so often to correct something that wasn't quite right. That afternoon, at Eagles practice, he was surprised to hear Sam compliment him on his own shooting form.

"Not that it was bad before," Sam hastened

to add. "But your shot just looks smoother and more consistent today."

It suddenly occurred to Tim that Peter, Red, and Keanu weren't the only ones benefiting from the mentoring program. Every time he explained how to do something to them, he was reminding himself how to do it. Now, whenever he caught himself doing a move wrong in practice, he corrected himself.

He mentioned his discovery to Dick a few days later during a water break. Dick grinned. "So you figured that out, huh? Good for you. Think Mike has learned the same thing?"

Tim thought about the way Mike yelled at his kids and shrugged. "Truthfully? No. But then again, he's probably teaching his crew a whole lot more than I'm teaching mine."

Dick drained his cup. "Guess we'll see during the demonstration on Parent Pickup Day next week."

Tim, in mid-sip, sputtered and choked. He had forgotten all about the demonstration!

14

With the demonstration suddenly looming over his head, Tim made a vow to teach Red, Peter, and Keanu an honest-to-goodness play the following morning. But a torrential rainstorm shut down all outdoor activities the next day. Tim didn't meet with his mentees, and the Eagles had only a short indoor practice so other teams could use the gymnasium.

At the end of the session, Tito announced the starting lineup against Camp Chickasaw. When Tim heard his name called along with Donnie, Brian, Cue Ball, and Mike, he had to clamp his lips shut to keep from shouting in triumph.

He'd set a goal to start on the court, not the bench—and he'd reached it!

His triumph was short-lived, however.

"You better not blow it for us *this* summer, Daniels," Mike growled as they passed each other. "I want a win."

Because of Tim's missed foul shot at the end of the game last summer, Chickasaw had ended Wickasaukee's ten-year undefeated record. When the Chickasaw bus rolled into the camp the next morning, it was clear from the chants and shouts that the visitors were looking to add another hash mark in their win column.

But Wickasaukee was just as determined to regain their lost crown.

Competitions of all sorts took place from after breakfast to lunch and then from lunch until dinner. Tim took part in a three-inning softball match that Wicky won, a water balloon toss that left him soaked to the skin when Billy flung the missile too hard, and the hundred-yard dash that saw him placing second overall. But as always, the highlight of the day was the much-anticipated boys' basketball showdown.

Tim had butterflies in his stomach as he joined the other Eagles on the court. Today they were all dressed in the camp's light blue and white jerseys with dark blue shorts. The Chickasaw players wore dark green uniforms. The two teams warmed up for fifteen minutes, and then the starters headed onto the floor.

Both teams were playing a half-court man-to-man defense. Tim identified who he'd be covering and then took his position for the tip-off. A moment later, the whistle blew, the ball was tossed up between the centers—and the game began!

Donnie was at center. He leaped and batted the ball into Mike's hands. Mike dribbled a few steps. Then his defender jumped in front of him, hands waving.

Tim dodged free of his man in case Mike looked to pass. But Mike hadn't lost his dribble. Rather than pass, he feinted to the right, switched hands, and tried to slip past the defense to the left.

The defender wasn't fooled. He dogged Mike every step, snaking his hand in so often that Mike finally stopped just outside the three-point arc.

He needs help! Tim darted toward his teammate, hands up.

But Mike didn't pass; he shot. His defender jumped with him and—*boom!*—walloped the ball straight down! A Chickasaw player moved to grab it off the bounce, but Tim was faster. He nabbed the ball, put it on the floor, and dribbled into the paint. Out of the corner of his eye, he saw Cue Ball slide into position under the basket. Without missing a beat, Tim directed a pass into his waiting hands. Cue Ball went up—score!

"A beautiful play by Tim Daniels, and

Wickasaukee gets on the board first," a voice over the loudspeaker bellowed. Tim glanced over and saw Dick Dunbar grinning from behind the microphone.

Tim raced back on defense, turning to jog backward when he crossed the half-court line. It was a good thing he did, too, because his man was bringing the ball down at top speed. If he'd still been facing the hoop, the guard would have blown by him for sure!

Shield popped into his head. He dropped into his low defensive stance, arms out. *Laser vision!* He kept his eyes trained on the man's midsection. When the guard stutter-stepped, Tim stuck with him instead of moving out of position.

The Chickasaw player passed the ball to a teammate. Mike dove for the steal but missed. Now his man had an open path to the hoop. He drove in and went up. Missed!

The Chickasaw fans groaned and the Wickasaukee fans cheered. Bobby Last came down with the rebound. He fired an outlet pass to Mike, who dribbled madly toward the hoop. Tim was sure he was going to go all the way, but at the last second he dished to Donnie, who was waiting at the low post. Donnie caught the pass at his chest and jumped with the ball.

Slap! Fweet!

Play stopped at the sound of the whistle. The referee tapped his arm to indicate that Donnie had been fouled, reported the offender's number to the table, and sent Donnie, whose shot had missed, to the line to shoot two.

Donnie sank them both. Wickasaukee, 4, Chickasaw, 0.

Two minutes later, Chickasaw drained one from the corner of the key to make it 4–2. Tim inbounded the ball to Mike. Mike took his time getting across half-court and then called out, "Twenty-two!"

Twenty-two was their standard pick play. Cue Ball ran to the top of the key and set himself sideways. Meanwhile, Mike sped up, drawing his defender with him—and smack into Cue Ball. Now free of his man, Mike took the ball to the hoop and laid it in for two more points.

"Mi-i-i-ke Gru-u-u-ber!" Dick drawled in perfect imitation of a professional announcer, eliciting laughter from the audience.

Back and forth the play went, with the score mounting steadily on both sides of the board. Yet try as they might, Chickasaw couldn't gain the lead. By halftime, they were eight points in the hole to Wickasaukee.

Tim had contributed two of his team's 32 points and had stolen the ball twice. He'd played most of the entire first half, too, and so wasn't too disappointed when Tito put Sam in to start the second half.

Mike, on the other hand, protested when Tito subbed Elijah for him. "Pipe down, Gruber," Tito snapped. "If you look closely, you'll see every starter's been replaced."

"But if we want to win—"

"Then we'll do it as a team," Jody interjected. "A *whole* team, not just a handful of players."

Mike looked as if he wanted to argue more. But Tito and Jody simply ignored him.

Tim couldn't believe it. Mike Gruber was their golden boy. What, he wondered, had happened to change that?

15

The players coming off the bench for Wickasaukee were fired up from watching their teammates take control of the game. Maybe they weren't quite as skilled as the starting five, but they were every bit as determined to give their team the win.

Unfortunately, their determination wasn't good enough to keep them on top. Tito sent the starters back in when the score turned in Chickasaw's favor, 49–45.

"I knew it," Mike spat. "All our hard work—gone!"

Tim glanced at the other players to see whom Mike was talking to. But as far as he could tell, none of them agreed with Mike's comment. And when Jody replaced Mike with Sam after five minutes, none of them seemed too upset.

"He got yanked because he was hogging the ball instead of setting up plays," Sam informed Tim during a time-out. "So if we want to stay in—"

"We better make something happen!" Tim finished. They bumped fists and got ready for play to resume.

Chickasaw had put in a new guard, a lefty who dribbled only with his dominant hand. Tim was so focused on staying with the guard that he didn't see the pick until it was almost too late. But he did see him, and so instead of colliding, he slipped behind the forward and picked up his man on the other side.

Brian Kelly was there, too. He and Tim slapped on the double-team, forcing the guard to pass. Sam anticipated the move, intercepted the ball, and took off all alone toward the other end of the court.

"Go, Sam! Go!" Tim shouted as he followed. If Sam got into trouble, he needed to be there to help.

But Sam didn't need any help. Cool as a cucumber, he banked in a soft layup.

"Sammy Sam," Cue Ball yelled, "you just earned yourself a ticket on the wahoo train! Wa-*hooooooo!* Chug-a-chug-a-chug-a!"

Wickasaukee was still down by two points, 57–55, when Brian made one of two foul shots. Then Chickasaw's lefty guard tossed in a three-pointer that swished the strings and drew cries of admiration from the fans from both camps.

Chickasaw, 60, Wickasaukee, 56.

Tito called a time-out to break their opponent's momentum and to urge his players to take more shots. "You're playing good D," he said, "but to win, you need to put the ball through the hoop. It's as simple as that."

It might have been simple, but it wasn't easy. Chickasaw subbed in fresh players but kept their hot-handed guard on the floor. Tim was so busy defending him that he had little time to think about shooting.

Meanwhile, the game clock ticked down and the score ticked up until with only two minutes remaining, it was knotted at 65 points apiece. Mike came back into the game. Now all five starters were playing.

"Full court man-to-man!" Jody ordered from the sideline. "Shut 'em down out there!"

Tim inbounded the ball to Mike from the mid-court sideline. Mike dribbled a few steps right-handed, passed the ball behind his back, and dribbled to the arc left-handed. Under the basket, Cue Ball feinted to the outside and then cut in, wide open and arms raised for a pass.

There was no way Mike could miss seeing him. But instead of passing, he set his feet and went up for a jumper.

Clang!

The ball bounced off the rim and landed

right in the hands of the surprised Chickasaw center. He looked around wildly for a guard to pass to. When he didn't see one, he put the ball to the floor himself. He was very tall; maybe that's why his dribble was so high. Cue Ball took advantage and swiped the ball from him. The center took two more steps before he realized he no longer had control.

Cue Ball, meanwhile, shot a layup. Rather than drop through the hoop, however, the ball rolled crazily around and around the rim—and fell off without going in!

Cue Ball tried to get his own rebound, but the Chickasaw center took his revenge by stripping the ball right out of Cue Ball's hands. This time, he found a guard waiting for the outlet pass. The guard passed up to a forward, who hit a jump shot from twelve feet away.

Chickasaw, 67, Wickasaukee, 65, with a minute remaining. Sixty seconds was plenty of time to tie things up. But was it enough time to go ahead? Tim wasn't sure.

Once more, he inbounded the ball to Mike. Now Chickasaw hit them with a full-court press. Mike was an expert ball handler, but Tim could see he was feeling the pressure—if only because he rifled a pass to him!

Tim was so startled he almost fudged the catch. But he controlled the ball. With a quick head fake, he sent his defender in one direction while he went in the other. He looked for someone to pass to. Cue Ball, Donnie, and Brian were all covered. It was up to him to tie the game!

"Trust yourself, Tim!" he heard Billy yell from the bleachers. "You can do it!"

Tim dribbled to the top of the key. The player defending Cue Ball took a step toward him and then retreated back to Cue Ball. Tim stepped into the paint, set his feet, and shot.

The ball traced a beautiful arc toward the hoop. Tim held his breath as it hit the backboard. Too high! Instead of falling through the net, the ball bounced over it!

Donnie and the Chickasaw center fought for the rebound. The ball started to go out of bounds. Donnie scrambled after it. With a mighty sweep, he drilled it off the Chickasaw player's legs and out of bounds!

It was Wickasaukee's ball under their own hoop!

16

"Time-out!" Tito shouted, frantically slapping his palm onto his fingertips.

Fweet! The ref's whistle blew and both teams hustled off the court. Jody was already drawing a play on his small whiteboard. "We don't have a lot of time, so pay attention," he said urgently. He flipped the board around so they could all see the play.

"Donnie, Cue Ball, and Bobby line up shoulder to shoulder in that order on the side of the foul line closest to where the ball is being inbounded. Tim, you stand behind Bobby. Mike, you inbound the ball. Got it?"

The boys nodded.

"Mike starts the play with a slap on the ball. When the rest of you hear that, move! Bobby, you cut to the right of the hoop. Cue Ball, you fade back a few steps. Donnie, you cut to the left and outside. Tim, you cut left, too, but to the inside. Everybody put your hands up and shout as if you're the one getting the pass. Mike, you feed the ball to Tim."

"What?" Mike jabbed an outraged finger at Tim. "You're putting our last hope of sending the game into overtime into *his* hands? He's barely taken a shot all game!"

"Exactly," said Jody. "So they won't expect him to be the shooter, will they?" He turned to Tim. "Think you can do it?"

"Of course he can't!" Mike cried before Tim could answer. "He should inbound the ball! I'll take the shot!"

Tim stood up. "I don't think I can," he said. When Mike started to agree, he added in a firm voice, "I know I can." He stared at Mike. "You do your job. I'll do mine."

The referee called for time-in then, preventing any further discussion. The boys raced onto the court and lined up as Jody had instructed. Only when he was hidden behind the three taller boys did Tim realize how smart Jody's plan was. The defense would have trouble covering a man they couldn't see!

"Get ready," Donnie whispered.

Whack!

Mike slapped the ball. The Eagles exploded into action. Bobby darted to the right of the hoop. Cue Ball danced back. Donnie swung wide to the left. Tim arced inside Donnie's path and turned toward Mike.

Mike wasn't looking at him. He was looking at Bobby. Bobby was covered. His eyes shifted to Donnie. But Donnie was covered, too.

Give it to me! Tim screamed in his head. *Your five seconds are almost up!*

Finally, Mike glanced at Tim. The Chickasaw center must have been watching his eyes because suddenly, he left Donnie and took a step toward Tim. Mike directed a bounce pass in Tim's direction, but instead of hitting the ground, the ball hit the center's foot! It took a crazy hop.

"Ten! Nine! Eight!" The Chickasaw fans started counting down the final seconds—just as Tim snared the ball out of the air!

"Seven! Six!"

The center leaped forward, arms high and waving. There was no way Tim could shoot over him. Unless…

"Five! Four!"

Tim put the ball in his right hand down by his side and turned so his shoulders were lined up with the hoop.

"Three! Two!"

Tim swept the ball up over his shoulder in an arc, pushed off his right leg, and flicked his wrist to send the ball spiraling through the air toward the hoop. And at the same time—wham! The center smacked into Tim, landing on him like a ton of bricks!

Fweet!

As Tim crumpled to the floor, two things registered in his brain. One, he'd been fouled on the shot. And two—the ball didn't even touch the rim. It just swished through the center of the strings! Nothin' but net!

Blaaaaaaa!

The buzzer sounded a split second after the basket. The fans erupted in cheers and shouts. The Eagles cleared the bench to swarm Tim, who was still on the floor, dazed and overjoyed.

"Tim Daniels sinks a buzzer-beating, game-tying hook shot under pressure!" Dick called over the loudspeaker. "And he was fouled, so he'll go to the line to shoot one!"

Sam helped Tim to his feet. "You can do it," he said. The other boys echoed his encouragement. Then everyone but the starting five hurried back to the sidelines to watch.

The gym fell silent as Tim walked to the foul line. The referee checked on the players' positions to make sure no one's feet were over the line. "Shooting one," he informed them.

Then he handed the ball to Tim and stepped back.

A thousand thoughts flooded Tim's mind.

The game is tied, so it's okay if you miss!

Don't screw up like you did last year!

Air ball! Air ball!

Tim swallowed hard and spun the ball between his fingers, trying to clear his head and focus. He dribbled twice and spun the ball again. Then suddenly, a new thought spoke inside his head.

Hang time!

All nervousness left him. He dribbled one more time and then, with a small smile playing about his lips, he bent his knees, uncoiled, and shot.

It wasn't a perfect free throw, Tim later admitted. It could have used more arc and been better centered. But despite its flaws, it did

113

the trick. The ball bounced once and then fell through the hoop.

If the crowd had gone crazy when Tim stuck the hook shot, now it went positively insane! Thunderous applause shook the rafters. Tito and Jody hoisted Tim onto their shoulders and paraded him around the gym. They were so different in height that Tim had to hold on for dear life or else risk toppling to the floor. But he didn't care. He wasn't just on top of their shoulders.

He was on top of the world!

17

Camp Wickasaukee celebrated their victory that night with an all-you-can-eat sundae bar followed by an enormous bonfire on the waterfront. While many of his Eagle teammates goofed around or flirted with campers from the girls' camp, Tim was content to sit and watch the flames. He'd had plenty of excitement for one day and was happy to just be alone—although he didn't mind when Wanda joined him. In fact, he thought that was very, very nice.

The next morning, he woke with a flutter in his stomach. It was Parent Pickup Day for the youngest campers. In just a few hours, his mentees would be showcasing what they had learned from him in the past week. He hoped it was enough to satisfy their parents!

The demonstration was scheduled for ten thirty. Tim had asked Keanu, Red, and Peter to arrive fifteen minutes early so they could talk about what they were going to do. He himself got to the gymnasium at ten minutes after ten. He looked around for his mentees. They were nowhere in sight.

It's still early, he thought.

At ten twenty, Mike Gruber and his kids appeared and began to warm up. Shortly after that, parents started arriving. To Tim's surprise, Tito, Jody, and several campers, some from the Eagles Nest and some from other cabins, showed up and took seats. Wanda and Billy were among them. He didn't remember telling Wanda about the demonstration but figured he must have while sitting with her the night before.

Tim glanced at the clock. It was ten

twenty-five—and Keanu, Red, and Peter were still nowhere to be seen. He didn't begin to panic until the minute hand ticked onto the six, however.

It's ten thirty! Where are they? Should I go find them? Should I—

His thoughts were interrupted by a sudden fanfare over the loudspeakers. Then Dick Dunbar's voice boomed out.

"Good morning and welcome, parents!" he said. "Before we start the basketball demonstration, a few of the kids have a little something they'd like to say to their mentor." The microphone made a rustling sound as if being covered by a hand, yet a whisper escaped anyway.

"You guys ready?"

The answer must have been yes because all at once, a door at the back of the gym burst open. Dick strode out, holding the microphone in his good hand. Behind him were Peter, Red, and Keanu.

Tim closed his eyes. They were wearing their capes!

"Tim Daniels, can you come forward, please?" Dick called.

Flushed with embarrassment, Tim opened his eyes and moved to join them on the court.

Dick handed the microphone to Red. "Go ahead," he whispered encouragingly.

Red opened up a piece of paper and began to read from it. "Dear Tim," he said, "when we first met you, you yelled a lot. You made us do boring drills. We didn't like that, or you, very much."

A murmur rippled through the audience. Tim glanced up and saw a few parents frowning. Then he caught Wanda's eye. She gave him a thumbs-up and a reassuring smile.

Red passed the paper and microphone to Peter. "But then one morning," Peter continued, "you did something different. Instead of yelling, you laughed and made jokes. Instead of making us do drills, you made up games. Instead of being mean, you were fun!"

Keanu took over. "At the beginning, we *hated* basketball. But now, thanks to you"—he looked at Red and Peter, who joined in the final words—"we think basketball is the best!"

"And you're the best, too, Tim!" Keanu added. Then he returned the microphone to Dick, presented the paper to Tim, and said to Red and Peter, "Ready? One, two, three!"

The boys unfurled their capes and turned around. Peter had the letter T and the word WE'LL on his. Red had the letter I and the word MISS. And Keanu's cape had an M and YOU!

Unfortunately, Peter and Red were standing in the wrong order, so the capes spelled out ITM and read as MISS WE'LL YOU! While the audience laughed, the boys quickly rearranged themselves so their message was clear: TIM WE'LL MISS YOU!

Tim grinned broadly. He tried to thank them but couldn't. A lump in his throat made speech impossible.

When the applause had died down, Dick spoke into the microphone again. "Tim and Mike, it's time for your mentees to show their parents what they've learned. Since Tim's kids are already on the court, they'll go first." He handed the microphone to Tim.

The grin froze on Tim's face. *Hoo boy,* he thought, glancing at the boys in their capes. *This could be interesting!*

Mike obviously thought so, too. His lips curled in a sardonic smile as he leaned back against the bleachers, spread his arms out wide, and crossed his feet at the ankles. To those around him, he must have appeared re-laxed and ready to enjoy the show. To Tim, however, he looked like the cat who was about to swallow the canary—and Tim was the canary!

18

Tim's palms turned sweaty. He took a moment to hand the paper the kids had given him to Billy.

"You'll do great," Billy whispered. "Trust yourself, man!"

Tim returned to the floor and took the microphone. He cleared his throat a few times and wet his lips.

"Hi, everyone, I'm Tim Daniels," he said at last. "I've been working with Red, Peter, and Keanu for the past week. Although, um, I guess it's really been more like a couple of days because like they said, I spent the first few days just yelling at them.

"I might have gone on yelling at them, too," he continued, "if I hadn't remembered something Dick once said to me. He told me that if I could show the kids that basketball is fun, then they'd want to keep playing. That made a lot of sense to me. I mean, let's face it—if they hate the sport, they're not going to want to keep playing it, right? And it would stink if they gave it up because if you ask me, they all have the ability to be really good players."

He glanced over at Keanu, Red, and Peter. All three were beaming at him. Suddenly, any nervousness Tim had vanished. He turned off the microphone and put it aside. Then he gathered the boys into a huddle.

"Okay, are you guys ready to show 'em what you can do?"

The threesome nodded eagerly.

"Should we keep our capes on?" Red asked.

"Of course!" Tim replied, ruffling the boy's

bright thatch of hair. "You're superheroes, right?"

"Right!"

They broke apart. Tim faced the audience again and explained that to make the basketball sessions fun as well as informative, he'd devised different activities to help the boys learn defensive and offensive skills. Then he had the boys demonstrate each activity while he described each drill and its goal.

"The first one is called dribbling without dribbling," he said as he handed basketballs to the boys. "The boys held ice cream cones in their free hands on a really hot day. As they dribbled the ball, they watched their ice cream for signs of melting. The drill taught them to keep their eyes up instead of watching the ball and to hold their free arm up to block defenders."

"And we learned to lick the ice cream fast so it wouldn't drip onto our hands!" Peter added, drawing a laugh from the crowd.

As Tim went through the rest of the drills—the potato-passing games, hang time, shield, laser vision, and take off—he told the audience where he got his inspiration for them.

"Keanu was my superhero, so it was with him in mind that I made the capes," he said. "Peter always seemed to be hungry, so the ice cream cone drill was for him. And Red, well, he didn't like the heat—and neither did I! So that's why we practiced in the water sometimes."

When he was finished, the audience applauded long and loud. Tim ducked his head, suddenly shy, and took his seat in the stands next to Wanda and Billy. Wanda gave him a big hug, and Billy punched him lightly on the shoulder.

"That was awesome!" Billy whispered.

"You were awesome," Wanda added, tucking a strand of hair behind her ear and smiling into his eyes.

Tim's face reddened again—but in a good way. Then he turned his attention back to the court to watch Mike.

Mike flicked on the microphone. "Good afternoon, parents. That sure was entertaining, wasn't it? Well, I'm going to take things in a more serious direction now, because I take basketball very seriously. It might be just a game to some"—he cut his gaze at Tim, eyebrows raised—"but to me, it's nothing to laugh about."

He jabbed a finger at his mentees. "All right, you three, come out here."

The small boys hurried onto the court. Mike passed them each a ball. "Dribbling drill one," he ordered.

Obediently, the boys dribbled the balls from the center line to the end line, switched to their other hands, and dribbled back. As one, they stopped, held their balls under their arms, and looked at Mike expectantly.

They're waiting for the next command, Tim

realized with a touch of envy. *Mike's really got them under control. Pretty impressive.*

Yet as Tim watched the boys demonstrate their skills, he began to wonder if it was that impressive after all. Sure, Mike's mentees performed each task better than his had. But the expressions on their faces were so blank that they looked like robots going through programmed motions. There was no energy, no life—no fun!

Mike finished his demonstration fifteen minutes later to a smattering of polite applause. Dick said a few final words, thanking both Tim and Mike for their efforts and inviting the parents to the dining hall for refreshments.

Tim had barely gone a step when Red bounced up to him and grabbed his arm. "Come on, you've got to meet my mom and dad!" he said, tugging Tim excitedly toward a young couple. Tim would have picked out Red's mother in a second, for her son had inherited her bright hair.

"My folks want to meet you, too!" Peter echoed.

"And mine!" Keanu put in.

"Okay, okay!" Tim said, laughing. A moment later, he was surrounded by six adults, all of whom were telling him how happy they were with his mentoring job.

"They made it easy because they were so enthusiastic," Tim confessed. "They're great kids. I'm going to miss them."

And to his surprise, he realized it was true. He wouldn't have believed it a week earlier, but he was going to miss spending time with the three little guys!

19

Before they made their way to the dining hall, Red, Peter, and Keanu's parents insisted that Tim pose for photos with their children.

"We'll send you copies the minute we get home," they promised. Then they all went together to share in the refreshments.

Mike was already at the dining hall, helping himself to cookies and juice. A few parents nodded to him, but no one approached him with a camera and none of his kids asked him to sit with them. When Tim looked for him again, Mike was gone.

Tim would never have thought it possible,

but he found himself feeling sorry for Mike Gruber.

The feeling didn't last long. The Eagles Nest campers played a pickup game that afternoon. On the first possession, Tim was bringing the ball down the court when Mike jumped in front of him and tried to swat the ball out of his hands.

He failed miserably because Tim knew from experience that that's what he'd do. So when Mike came at him at the top of the key, Tim turned his shoulders to the hoop as if setting up for a hook shot.

"Don't have any other moves, huh, Daniels?" Mike taunted as Tim jumped.

"Oh, don't I?" Tim responded—and instead of shooting at the top of his arc, he fired an over-the-head pass to Donnie, who converted it into two points.

Mike clamped his mouth shut in a tight line and gave Tim a dirty look. But he didn't say anything else to him for the rest of the game.

The stony silence between them might have continued indefinitely if Tim hadn't decided to break it.

"Listen, you don't like me, and I don't like you," he told Mike at a campfire a few nights later, "but it looks like we're going to be in the starting lineup together for the next inter-camp game. So, for the good of the team, let's keep our differences off the court. Deal?"

He stuck out his hand, half expecting Mike to snort and push it aside.

After a moment's hesitation, though, the other boy shook it. "Deal," Mike said.

Their truce was an uneasy one, but in time, they began to play together better. Their improved communication made the team better as a whole, allowing them to win their third and final inter-camp game by more than ten points.

And as the days passed, a funny thing happened. Their camaraderie on the court spilled into their lives off the court. While

Tim knew he and Mike would never have the kind of friendship he and Billy had, they were no longer enemies—at least for this summer.

Whether they would pick up where they left off next summer remained to be seen!

Tim and Billy returned home two weeks later. Billy had earned his junior lifeguarding certificate. On the car ride home, he talked about returning to Camp Wickasaukee the next summer so he could go for his senior certification.

Tim had burst out laughing. "Next summer? We haven't finished this one yet! There's a whole month left to go, and I've got big plans."

Those plans included plenty of basketball, plus pool time, video games, and going to the movies with Wanda—with other friends along, too, of course. After all, he insisted when Billy teased him, it wasn't like they were boyfriend and girlfriend!

But before anything of those things, Tim had something important to do when he got home. First, he mounted a wooden shelf he had made at the arts and crafts center on the wall in his room. (Now that Gruber the clown puppet was no longer there, he found he didn't mind spending time at the center. That Wanda liked to go there had nothing to do with it.)

Then he bought a big picture frame with lots of openings for photos. He filled the smaller openings with the photos his mentees' parents had sent him. He added a few of his own photos, too, including one of Billy jumping off the end of the dock.

In one of two bigger openings, he put the letter Keanu, Red, and Peter had read at the demonstration. The second big space was for his favorite photo. It showed him kneeling and hugging his mentees. The boys had their capes to the camera, so the message TIM WE'LL MISS YOU! was clearly visible.

Dick Dunbar was in the shot, too, standing to one side with a huge smile on his face. He had written a note across the bottom of the picture.

To my buddy Tim, his message read, *Never forget: Take that pizza one slice at a time!* He'd signed it in a big loopy scrawl.

Tim set the frame onto the shelf and stood back to admire it. Then, with a smile playing about his lips, he pretended to shoot a hook shot.

"Swish," he whispered. Then he posed for a free throw and shot that, too. "And one! Tim Daniels is a hook shot hero!"

MATT CHRISTOPHER

THE #1 SPORTS SERIES FOR KIDS ®

Read them all!

*Previously published as *Crackerjack Halfback*

All available in paperback from Little, Brown and Company
**Previously published as *Baseball Pals*

Matt Christopher®

Muhammad Ali

Kobe Bryant

Dale Earnhardt Sr.

Jeff Gordon

Tony Hawk

Dwight Howard

LeBron James

Derek Jeter

Michael Jordan

Peyton and Eli Manning

Shaquille O'Neal

Albert Pujols

Jackie Robinson

Alex Rodriguez

Babe Ruth

Tiger Woods